A Village Stra

Kate Douglas Smith Wiggin

Alpha Editions

This edition published in 2024

ISBN : 9789362995117

Design and Setting By
Alpha Editions
www.alphaedis.com
Email - info@alphaedis.com

As per information held with us this book is in Public Domain.
This book is a reproduction of an important historical work. Alpha Editions uses the best technology to reproduce historical work in the same manner it was first published to preserve its original nature. Any marks or number seen are left intentionally to preserve its true form.

Contents

I .... - 1 -
II .... - 8 -
III .... - 12 -
IV .... - 17 -
V .... - 21 -
VI .... - 28 -

I

> "Goodfellow, Puck and goblins,
> Know more than any book.
> Down with your doleful problems,
> And court the sunny brook.
> The south-winds are quick-witted,
> The schools are sad and slow,
> The masters quite omitted
> The lore we care to know."
>
> EMERSON'S *April*.

"FIND the three hundred and seventeenth page, Davy, and begin at the top of the right-hand column."

The boy turned the leaves of the old instruction book obediently, and then began to read in a sing-song, monotonous tone:

"'One of Pag-pag'"—

"Pag-a-ni-ni's"

"'One of Paggernyner's' (I wish all the fellers in your stories didn't have such tough old names!) 'most dis-as-ter-ous triumphs he had when playing at Lord Holland's.' (Who was Lord Holland, uncle Tony?) 'Some one asked him to im-provise on the violin the story of a son who kills his father, runs a-way, becomes a high-way-man, falls in love with a girl who will not listen to him; so he leads her to a wild country site, suddenly jumping with her from a rock into an a-b-y-s-s'"

"Abyss."

"'—a—rock—into—an—abyss, where they disappear for ever. Paggernyner listened quietly, and when the story was at an end he asked that all the lights should be distinguished.'"

"Look closer, Davy."

"'Should be *ex*tinguished. He then began playing, and so terrible was the musical in-ter-pre-ta-tion of the idea which had been given him that several of the ladies fainted, and the sal-salon-s*a*lon, when relighted, looked like a battle-field.' Cracky! Wouldn't you like to have been there, uncle Tony? But I don't believe anybody ever played that way, do you?"

"Yes," said the listener, dreamily raising his sightless eyes to the elm-tree that grew by the kitchen door. "I believe it, and I can hear it myself when you read the story to me. I feel that the secret of everything in the world that is beautiful, or true, or terrible, is hidden in the strings of my violin, Davy, but only a master can draw it from captivity."

"You make stories on your violin, too, uncle Tony, even if the ladies don't faint away in heaps, and if the kitchen doesn't look like a battle-field when you've finished. I'm glad it doesn't, for my part, for I should have more housework to do than ever."

"Poor Davy! you couldn't hate housework any worse if you were a woman; but it is all done for to-day. Now paint me one of your pictures, laddie; make me see with your eyes."

The boy put down the book and leaped out of the open door, barely touching the old millstone that served for a step. Taking a stand in the well-worn path, he rested his hands on his hips, swept the landscape with the glance of an eagle, and began like a young improvisator:

"The sun is just dropping behind Brigadier Hill."

"What colour is it?"

"Red as fire, and there isn't anything near it—it's almost alone in the sky; there's only teeny little white feather clouds here and there. The bridge looks as if it was a silver string tying the two sides of the river together. The water is pink where the sun shines into it. All the leaves of the trees are kind of swimming in the red light—I tell you, nunky, just as if I was looking through red glass. The weather vane on Squire Bean's barn dazzles so the rooster seems to be shooting gold arrows into the river. I can see the tip top of Mount Washington where the peak of its snow-cap touches the pink sky. The hen-house door is open. The chickens are all on their roost, with their heads cuddled under their wings."

"Did you feed them?"

The boy clapped his hand over his mouth with a comical gesture of penitence, and dashed into the shed for a panful of corn, which he scattered over the ground, enticing the sleepy fowls by insinuating calls of "Chick, chick, chick, chick! *Come*, biddy, biddy, biddy, biddy! *Come*, chick, chick, chick, chick, chick!"

The man in the doorway smiled as over the misdemeanour of somebody very dear and lovable, and rising from his chair felt his way to a corner shelf, took down a box, and drew from it a violin swathed in a silk bag. He removed the covering with reverential hands. The tenderness of his face was like that of a young mother dressing or undressing her child. As he fingered the instrument his hands seemed to have become all eyes. They wandered caressingly over the polished surface as if enamoured of the perfect thing that they had created, lingering here and there with rapturous tenderness on some special beauty—the graceful arch of the neck, the melting curves of the cheeks, the delicious swell of the breasts.

When he had satisfied himself for the moment, he took the bow, and lifting the violin under his chin, inclined his head fondly toward it and began to play.

The tone at first seemed muffled, but had a curious bite, that began in distant echoes, but after a few minutes' playing grew firmer and clearer, ringing out at last with velvety richness and strength until the atmosphere was satiated with harmony. No more ethereal note ever flew out of a bird's throat than Anthony Croft set free from this violin, his *liebling*, his "swan song," made in the year he had lost his eyesight.

Anthony Croft had been the only son of his mother, and she a widow. His boyhood had been exactly like that of all the other boys in Edgewood, save that he hated school a trifle more, if possible, than any of the others; though there was a unanimity of aversion in this matter that surprised and wounded teachers and parents.

The school was the ordinary district school of that time; there were not enough scholars for what Cyse Higgins called a "degraded" school. The difference between Anthony and the other boys lay in the reason for as well as the degree of his abhorrence.

He had come into the world a naked, starving human soul; he longed to clothe himself, and he was hungry and ever hungrier for knowledge; but never within the four walls of the village schoolhouse could he seize hold of one fact that would yield him its secret sense, one glimpse of clear light that would shine in upon the darkness of his mind, one thought or word that would feed his soul.

The only place where his longings were ever stilled, where he seemed at peace with himself, where he understood what he was made for, was out of doors in the woods. When he should have been poring over the sweet, palpitating mysteries of the multiplication table, his vagrant gaze was always on the open window near which he sat. He could never study when a fly buzzed on the window-pane; he was always standing on the toes of his bare feet, trying to locate and understand the buzz that puzzled him. The book was a mute, soulless thing that had no relation to his inner world of thought and feeling. He turned ever from the dead seven-times-six to the mystery of life about him.

He was never a special favourite with his teachers; that was scarcely to be expected. In his very early years, his pockets were gone through with every morning when he entered the school door, and the contents, when confiscated, would comprise a jew's-harp, a bit of catgut, screws whittled out of wood, tacks, spools, pins, and the like. But when robbed of all these he could generally secrete a fragment of india-rubber drawn from an old pair of suspenders, and this, when put between his teeth and stretched to its utmost capacity, would yield a delightful twang when played upon with the forefinger. He could also fashion an interesting musical instrument in his desk by means of spools and catgut and bits of broken glass. The chief joy of his life was an old tuning-fork that the teacher of the singing-school had given him, but, owing to the degrading and arbitrary censorship of pockets that prevailed, he never dared bring it into the schoolroom. There were ways, however, of evading inexorable law and circumventing base injustice. He hid the precious thing under a thistle just outside the window. The teacher had sometimes a brief season of apathy on hot afternoons, when she was hearing the primer class read, "*I see a pig. The pig is big. The big pig can dig*"; which stirring phrases were always punctuated by the snores of the Hanks baby, who kept sinking down on his fat little legs in the line and giving way to slumber during the lesson. At such a moment Anthony slipped out of the window and snapped the tuning-fork several times—just enough to save his soul from death—and then slipped in again. He was caught occasionally, but not often; and even when he was, there were mitigating circumstances, for he was generally put under the teacher's desk for punishment. It was a dark close, sultry spot, but when he was well seated, and had grown tired of looking at the triangle of black elastic in the teacher's "congress" shoe, and tired of wishing it was his instead of hers, he would tie one end of a bit of thread to the button of his gingham shirt, and, carrying it round his left ear several times, make believe he was Paganini languishing in prison and playing on a violin with a single string.

As he grew older there was no marked improvement, and Tony Croft was by general assent counted the laziest boy in the village. That he was lazy in certain matters merely because he was in a frenzy of industry to pursue certain others had nothing to do with the case, of course.

If any one had ever given him a task in which he could have seen cause working to effect, in which he could have found by personal experiment a single fact that belonged to him, his own by divine right of discovery, he would have counted labour or study all joy.

He was one incarnate Why and How; one brooding wonder and interrogation point. "Why does the sun drive away the stars? Why do the leaves turn red and gold? What makes the seed swell in the earth? From whence comes the life hidden in the egg under the bird's breast? What holds the moon in the sky? Who regulates her shining? Who moves the wind? Who made me, and what am I? Who, why, how, whither? If I came from God but only lately, teach me his lessons first, put me into vital relation with life and law, and then give me your dead signs and equivalents for real things, that I may learn more and more, and ever more and ever more." These were the questions his eager soul was always asking of the outer world.

There was no spirit in Edgewood bold enough to conceive that Tony learned anything in the woods, but as there was never sufficient school money to keep the village seat of learning open more than half the year, the boy educated himself at the fountain head of wisdom and knowledge the other half. His mother, who owned him for a duckling hatched from a hen's egg, and was never quite sure he would not turn out a black sheep and a crooked stick to boot, was obliged to confess that Tony had more useless information than any boy in the village. He knew just where to find the first Mayflowers, and would bring home the waxen beauties when other people had scarcely begun to think about the spring. He could tell where to look for the rare fringed gentian, the yellow violet, the Indian pipe. There were clefts in the high rocks by the river side where, when every one else failed, he could find harebells and columbines.

When his tasks were done, and the other boys were amusing themselves each in his own way, you would find Tony lying flat on the pine-needles in the woods, listening to the notes of the wild birds, and imitating them patiently, till you could scarcely tell which was boy and which was bird; and if you could, the birds couldn't, for many a time he coaxed the bobolinks and thrushes to perch on the low boughs above his head, where they chirped to him as if he were a feathered brother. There was nothing about the building of nests with which he was not familiar. He could have helped in the task, if the birds had not been so shy, and if he had possessed beak and claw instead of clumsy fingers. He would sit near a beehive for hours without moving, or lie prone in the sandy road, under the full glare of the sun, watching the ants acting out their human comedy; sometimes surrounding a favourite hill with stones, that the comedy might not be turned into tragedy by a careless footfall. The cottage on the river road grew more and more to resemble a museum and herbarium as the years went by, and the Widow Croft's weekly house-cleaning was a matter that called for the exercise of Christian grace.

Still, Tony was a good son, affectionate, considerate, and obedient. His mother had no idea that he would ever be able, or indeed willing, to make a living; but there was a forest of young timber growing up, a small hay farm to depend upon, and a little hoard that would keep him out of the poorhouse when she died and left him to his own devices. It never occurred to her that he was in any way remarkable. If he were difficult to understand, it reflected more upon his eccentricity than upon her density. What was a woman to do with a boy of twelve who, when she urged him to drop the old guitar he was taking apart and hurry off to school, cried, "Oh, mother! when there is so much to learn in this world, it is wicked, wicked, to waste time in school."

About this period Tony spent hours in the attic arranging bottles and tumblers into a musical scale. He also invented an instrument made of small and great, long and short pins, driven into soft board to different depths, and when the widow passed his door on the way to bed she invariably saw this barbaric thing locked to the boy's breast, for he often played himself to sleep with it.

At fifteen he had taken to pieces and put together again, strengthened, soldered, mended, and braced, every accordion, guitar, melodeon, dulcimer, and fiddle in Edgewood, Pleasant River, and the neighbouring villages. There was a little money to be earned in this way, but very little, as people in general regarded this "tinkering" as a pleasing diversion in which they could indulge him without danger. As an example of this attitude, Dr. Berry's wife's melodeon had lost two stops, the pedals had severed connection with the rest of the works, it wheezed like an asthmatic, and two black keys were missing. Anthony worked more than a week on its rehabilitation, and received in return Mrs. Berry's promise that the doctor would "pull a tooth" for him some time! This, of course, was a guerdon for the future, but it seemed pathetically distant to the lad who had never had a toothache in his life. He had to plead with Cyse Higgins for a week before that prudent young farmer would allow him to touch his five-dollar fiddle. He obtained permission at last only by offering to give Cyse his calf in case he spoiled the violin. "That seems square," said Cyse doubtfully, "but after all, you can't play on a calf!" "Neither will your fiddle give milk, if you keep it long enough," retorted Tony; and this argument was convincing.

So great was his confidence in Tony's skill that Squire Bean trusted his father's violin to him, one that had been bought in Berlin seventy years before. It had been hanging on the attic wall for a half-century, so that the back was split in twain, the sound-post lost, the neck and the tailpiece cracked. The lad took it home, and studied it for two whole evenings before the open fire. The problem of restoring it was quite beyond his abilities. He finally took the savings of two summers' "blueberry money" and walked sixteen miles to the nearest town, where he bought a book called "The Practical Violinist." The supplement proved to be a mine of wealth. Even the headings appealed to his imagination and intoxicated him with their suggestions—On Scraping, Splitting, and Repairing Violins, Violin Players, Great Violinists, Solo Playing, &c.; and at the very end a Treatise on the Construction, Preservation, Repair, and Improvement of the Violin, by Jacob Augustus Friedheim, Instrument Maker to the Court of the Archduke of Weimar.

There was a good deal of moral advice in the preface that sadly puzzled the boy, who was always in a condition of chronic amazement at the village disapprobation of his favourite fiddle. That the violin did not in some way receive the confidence enjoyed by other musical instruments, he perceived from various paragraphs written by the worthy author of "The Practical Violinist," as for example:

"Some very excellent Christian people hold a strong prejudice against the violin because they have always known it associated with dancing and dissipation. Let it be understood that your violin is 'converted,' and such an objection will no longer lie against it . . . Many delightful hours may be enjoyed by a young man, if he has obtained a respectable knowledge of his instrument, who otherwise would find the time hang heavy on his hands; or, for want of some better amusement, would frequent the dangerous and destructive paths of vice and be ruined for ever. I am in hopes, therefore, my dear young pupil, that your violin will occupy your attention at just those very times when, if you were immoral or dissipated, you would be at the grogshop, gaming-table, or among vicious females. Such a use of the violin, notwithstanding the prejudices many hold against it, must contribute to virtue, and furnish abundance of innocent and entirely unobjectionable amusement. These are the views with which I hope you have adopted it, and will continue to cherish and cultivate it."

II

> "There is no bard in all the choir,
> . . . .
> Not one of all can put in verse,
> Or to this presence could rehearse
> The sights and voices ravishing
> The boy knew on the hills in spring,
> When pacing through the oaks he heard
> Sharp queries of the sentry-bird,
> The heavy grouse's sudden whir,
> The rattle of the kingfisher."
>
> EMERSON'S *Harp*.

NOW began an era of infinite happiness, of days that were never long enough, of evenings when bedtime came all too soon. Oh, that there had been some good angel who would have taken in hand Anthony Croft the boy, and, training the powers that pointed so unmistakably in certain directions, given to the world the genius of Anthony Croft, potential instrument maker to the court of St. Cecilia; for it was not only that he had the fingers of a wizard; his ear caught the faintest breath of harmony or hint of discord, as

> "Fairy folk a-listening
> Hear the seed sprout in the spring,
> And for music to their dance
> Hear the hedge-rows wake from trance;
> Sap that trembles into buds
> Sending little rhythmic floods
> Of fairy sound in fairy ears.
> Thus all beauty that appears
> Has birth as sound to finer sense
> And lighter-clad intelligence."

As the universe is all mechanism to one man, all form and colour to another, so to Anthony Croft the world was all melody. Notwithstanding these many gifts and possibilities, the doctor's wife advised the Widow Croft to make a plumber of him, intimating delicately that these freaks of nature, while playing no apparent part in the divine economy, could sometimes be made self-supporting.

The seventeenth year of his life marked a definite epoch in his development. He studied Jacob Friedheim's treatise until he knew the characteristics of all the great violin models, from the Amatis, Hieronymus, Antonius, and Nicolas, to those of Stradivarius, Guarnerius, and Steiner.

It was in this year, also, that he made a very precious discovery. While browsing in the rubbish in Squire Bean's garret to see if he could find the missing sound-post of the old violin, he came upon a billet of wood wrapped in cloth and paper. When unwrapped, it was plainly labelled "Wood from the Bean Maple at Pleasant Point; the biggest maple in York County, and believed to be one of the biggest in the State of Maine." Anthony found that the oldest inhabitant of Pleasant River remembered the stump of the tree, and that the boys used to jump over it and admire its proportions whenever they went fishing at the Point. The wood, therefore, was perhaps eighty or ninety years old. The squire agreed willingly that it should be used to mend the ancient violin, and told Tony he should have what was left for himself. When, by careful calculation, he found that the remainder would make a whole violin, he laid it reverently away for another twenty years, so that he should be sure it had completed its century of patient waiting for service, and falling on his knees by his bedside said, "I thank Thee, Heavenly Father, for this precious gift, and I promise from this moment to gather the most beautiful wood I can find, and lay it by where it can be used some time to make perfect violins, so that if any creature as poor and as helpless as I am needs the wherewithal to do good work, I shall have helped him as Thou hast helped me." And according to his promise so he did, and the pieces of richly curled maple, of sycamore, and of spruce began to accumulate. They were cut from the sunny side of the trees, in just the right season of the year, split so as to have a full inch thickness towards the bark, and a quarter-inch towards the heart. They were then laid for weeks under one of the falls in Wine Brook, where the musical tinkle, tinkle of the stream fell on the wood already wrought upon by years of sunshine and choruses of singing birds.

This boy, toiling not alone for himself, but with full and conscious purpose for posterity also, was he not worthy to wear the mantle of Antonius Stradivarius?

> "That plain white-aproned man who stood at work
> Patient and accurate full fourscore years,
> Cherished his sight and touch by temperance
> And since keen sense is love of perfectness,
> Made perfect violins, the needed paths
> For inspiration and high mastery."

And as if the year were not full enough of glory, the school-teacher sent him a book with a wonderful poem in it.

That summer's teaching had been the freak of a college student, who had gone back to his senior year strengthened by his experience of village life. Anthony Croft, who was only three or four years his junior, had been his favourite pupil and companion.

"How does Tony get along?" asked the Widow Croft when the teacher came to call.

"Tony? Oh, I can't teach him anything."

Tears sprang to the mother's eyes.

"I know he ain't much on book learning," she said apologetically, "but I'm bound he don't make you no trouble in deportment."

"I mean," said the school-teacher gravely, "that I can show him how to read a little Latin and do a little geometry, but he knows as much in one day as I shall ever know in a year."

Tony crouched by the old fireplace in the winter evenings, dropping his knife or his compasses a moment to read aloud to his mother, who sat in the opposite corner knitting:

> "Of old Antonio Stradivari—him
> Who a good century and a half ago
> Put his true work in the brown instrument,
> And by the nice adjustment of its frame
> Gave it responsive life, continuous
> With the master's finger-tips, and perfected
> Like them by delicate rectitude of use."

The mother listened with painful intentness. "I like the sound of it," she said, "but I can't hardly say I take in the full sense."

"Why, mother," said the lad, in a rare moment of self-expression, "you know the poetry says he cherished his sight and touch by temperance; that an idiot might see a straggling line and be content, but he had an eye that winced at false work, and loved the true. When it says his finger-tips were perfected by delicate rectitude of use, I think it means doing everything as it is done in heaven, and that anybody who wants to make a perfect violin must keep his eye open to all the beautiful things God has made, and his ear open to all the music he has put into the world, and then never let his hands touch a piece of work that is crooked or straggling or false, till, after years and years of rightness, they are fit to make a violin like the squire's, a violin that can say everything, a violin that an angel wouldn't be ashamed to play on."

Do these words seem likely ones to fall from the lips of a lad who had been at the tail of his class ever since his primer days? Well, Anthony was seventeen now, and he was "educated," in spite of sorry recitations—educated, the Lord knows how! Yes, in point of fact the Lord does know how! He knows how the drill and pressure of the daily task, still more the presence of the high ideal, the inspiration working from within, how these educate us.

The blind Anthony Croft sitting in the kitchen doorway had seemingly missed the heights of life he might have trod, and had walked his close on fifty years through level meadows of mediocrity, a witch in every finger-tip waiting to be set to work, head among the clouds, feet stumbling, eyes and ears open to hear God's secret thought; seeing and hearing it, too, but lacking force to speak it forth again; for while imperious genius surmounts all obstacles, brushes laws and formulas from its horizon, and with its own free soul sees its "path and the outlets of the sky," potential genius for ever needs an angel of deliverance to set it free.

Poor Anthony Croft, or blessed Anthony Croft, I know not which—God knows! Poor he certainly was, yet blessed after all. "One thing I do," said Paul. "One thing I do," said Anthony. He was not able to realise his ideals, but he had the angel aim by which he idealised his reals.

O waiting heart of God! how soon would Thy kingdom come if we all did our allotted tasks, humble or splendid, in this consecrated fashion!

III

"Therein I hear the Parcæ reel
The threads of man at their humming wheel,
The threads of life and power and pain,
So sweet and mournful falls the strain."

EMERSON'S *Harp*.

OLD Mrs. Butterfield had had her third stroke of paralysis, and died of a Sunday night. She was all alone in her little cottage on the river bank, with no neighbour nearer than Croft's, and nobody there but a blind man and a small boy. Everybody had told her it was foolish for a frail old woman of seventy to live alone in a house on the river road, and everybody was pleased, in a discreet and chastened fashion of course, that it had turned out exactly as they had predicted.

Aunt Mehitable Tarbox was walking up to Milliken's Mills, with her little black reticule hanging over her arm, and noticing that there was no smoke coming out of the Butterfield chimney, and that the hens were gathered about the kitchen door clamouring for their breakfast, she thought it best to stop and knock. No response followed the repeated blows from her hard knuckles. She then tapped smartly on Mrs. Butterfield's bedroom window with her thimble finger. This proving of no avail, she was obliged to pry open the kitchen shutter, split open the screen of mosquito netting with her shears, and crawl into the house over the sink. This was a considerable feat for a somewhat rheumatic elderly lady, but this one never grudged trouble when she wanted to find out anything.

When she discovered that her premonitions were correct, and old Mrs. Butterfield was indeed dead, her grief at losing a pleasant acquaintance was largely mitigated by her sense of importance at being first on the spot, and chosen by Providence to take command of the situation. There were no relations in the village; there was no woman neighbour within a mile: it was therefore her obvious Christian duty not only to take charge of the "remains," but to conduct such a funeral as the remains would have wished for herself.

The fortunate Vice-President suddenly called upon by destiny to guide the ship of state, the soldier who sees a possible Victoria Cross in a hazardous engagement, can have a faint conception of Aunt Hitty's feeling on this momentous occasion. Funerals were the very breath of her life. There was no ceremony, either of public or private import, that, to her mind, approached a funeral in real satisfying interest. Yet, with distinct talent in this direction, she had always been "cabined, cribbed, confined" within hopeless limitations. She had assisted in a secondary capacity at funerals in the families of other people, but she would have revelled in personally conducted ones. The members of her own family stubbornly refused to die, however, even the distant connections living on and on to a ridiculous old age; and if they ever did die, by reason of a falling roof, shipwreck, or conflagration, they generally died in Texas or Iowa, or some remote State where Aunt Hitty could not follow the hearse in the first carriage. This blighted ambition was a heart-sorrow of so deep and sacred a character that she did not even confess it to "Si," as her appendage of a husband was called.

Now at last her chance for planning a funeral had come. Mrs. Butterfield had no kith or kin save her niece, Lyddy Ann, who lived in Andover, or Lawrence, or Haverhill, Massachusetts—Aunt Hitty couldn't remember which, and hoped nobody else could. The niece would be sent for when they found out where she lived; meanwhile the funeral could not be put off.

She glanced round the house preparatory to locking it up and starting to notify Anthony Croft. She would just run over and talk to him about ordering the coffin; then she could attend to all other necessary preliminaries herself. The remains had been well-to-do, and there was no occasion for sordid economy, so Aunt Hitty determined in her own mind to have the latest fashion in everything, including a silver coffin-plate. The Butterfield coffin-plates were a thing to be proud of. They had been sacredly preserved for years and years, and the entire collection—numbering nineteen in all—had been framed, and adorned the walls of the deceased lady's best room. They were not of solid silver, it is true, but even so it was a matter of distinction to have belonged to a family that could afford to have nineteen coffin-plates of any sort.

Aunt Hitty planned certain dramatic details as she walked down the road to Croft's. It came to her in a burst of inspiration that she would have two ministers: one for the long prayer, and one for the short prayer and the remarks. She hoped that Elder Weeks would be adequate in the latter direction. She knew she couldn't for the life of her think of anything interesting to say about Mrs. Butterfield, save that she possessed nineteen coffin-plates, and brought her hens to Edgewood every summer for their health; but she had heard Elder Weeks make a moving discourse out of less than that. To be sure, he needed priming, but she would be equal to the occasion. There was Ivory Brown's funeral: how would that have gone on if it hadn't been for her? Wasn't the elder ten minutes late, and what would his remarks have amounted to without her suggestions? You might almost say she was the author of the discourse, for she gave the elder all the appropriate ideas. As she had helped him out of the waggon she had said: "Are you prepared? I thought not; but there's no time to lose. Remember there are aged parents; two brothers living—one railroading in Spokane Falls, the other clerking in Washington, D.C. Don't mention the Universalists—there's be'n two in the fam'ly; nor insanity—there's be'n one o' them. The girl in the corner is the one that the remains has be'n keeping comp'ny with. If you can make some genteel allusions to her, it'll be much appreciated by his folks."

As to the long prayer, she knew that the Rev. Mr. Ford could be relied on to pray until Aunt Becky Burnham should twitch him by the coat-tails. She had done it more than once. She had also, on one occasion, got up and straightened his ministerial neckerchief, which he had gradually "prayed" around his saintly neck until it had lodged behind the right ear.

These plans proved so fascinating to Aunt Hitty that she walked quite half a mile beyond Croft's, and was obliged to retrace her steps. Meantime, she conceived bands of black alpaca for the sleeves and hats of the pall-bearers, and a festoon of the same over the front gate, if there should be any left over. She planned the singing by the choir. There had been no real choir-singing at any funeral in Edgewood since the Rev. Joshua Beckwith had died. She would ask them to open with—

This was a favourite funeral hymn. The only difficulty would be in keeping Aunt Becky Burnham from pitching it in a key where nobody but a soprano skylark, accustomed to warble at a great height, could possibly sing it. It was generally given at the grave, when Elder Weeks officiated; but it never satisfied Aunt Hitty, because the good elder always looked so unpicturesque when he threw a red bandanna handkerchief over his head before beginning the twenty-seven verses. After the long prayer, she would have Almira Berry give for a solo—

This hymn, if it did not wholly reconcile one to death, enabled one to look upon life with sufficient solemnity. It was a thousand pities, she thought, that the old hearse was so shabby and rickety, and that Gooly Eldridge, who drove it, would insist on wearing a faded peach-blow overcoat. It was exasperating to think of the public spirit at Egypt, and contrast it with the state of things at Pleasant River. In Egypt, they had sold the old hearse-house for a sausage-shop, and now they were having "hearse sociables" every month to raise money for a new one.

All these details flew through Aunt Hitty's mind in fascinating procession. There shouldn't be "a hitch" anywhere. There had been a hitch at her last funeral, but she had been only an assistant there. Matt Henderson had been struck by lightning at the foot of Squire Bean's old nooning tree, and certain circumstances combined to make the funeral one of unusual interest, so much so much so that fat old Mrs. Potter from Deerwander created a sensation at the cemetery. She was so anxious to get where she could see everything to the best advantage that she crowded too near the bier, stepped on the sliding earth, and pitched into the grave. As she weighed over two hundred pounds, and was in a position of some disadvantage, it took five men to extricate her from the dilemma, and the operation made a long and somewhat awkward break in the religious services. Aunt Hitty always said of this catastrophe, "If I'd 'a' be'n Mis' Potter, I'd 'a' be'n so mortified I believe I'd 'a' said, 'I wa'n't plannin' to be buried, but now I'm in here I declare I'll stop.'"

* * * * *

Old Mrs. Butterfield's funeral was not only voted an entire success by the villagers, but the seal of professional approval was set upon it by an undertaker from Saco, who declared that Mrs. Tarbox could make a handsome living in the funeral line anywhere. Providence, who always assists those who assist themselves, decreed that the niece Lyddy Ann should not arrive until the aunt was safely buried; so, there being none to resist her right or grudge her the privilege, Aunt Hitty, for the first time in her life, rode in the next buggy to the hearse. Si, in his best suit, a broad weed and weepers, drove Cyse Higgins' black colt, and Aunt Hitty was dressed in deep mourning, with the Widow Buzzell's crape veil over her face, and in her hand a palm-leaf fan tied with a black ribbon. Her comment to Si, as she went to her virtuous couch that night, was: "It was an awful dry funeral, but that was the only flaw in it. It would 'a' be'n perfect if there'd be'n anybody to shed tears. I come pretty nigh it myself, though I ain't no relation, when Elder Weeks said, 'You'll go round the house, my sisters, and Mis' Butterfield won't be there; you'll go int' the orchard, and Mis' Butterfield won't be there; you'll go int' the barn, and Mis' Butterfield won't be there; you'll go int' the shed, and Mis' Butterfield wont be there; you'll go int' the hencoop, and Mis' Butterfield won't be there!' That would 'a' draw'd tears from a stone, 'most, 'specially sence Mis' Butterfield set such store by her hens."

And this is the way that Lyddy Butterfield came into her kingdom, a little lone brown house on the river's brim. She had seen it only once before when she had drives, out from Portland, years ago, with her aunt. Mrs. Butterfield lived in Portland, but spent her summers in Edgewood on account of her chickens. She always explained that the country was dreadful dull for her, but good for the hens; they always laid so much better in the winter time.

Lyddy liked the place all the better for its loneliness. She had never had enough of solitude, and this quiet home, with the song of the river for company, if one needed more company than chickens and a cat, satisfied all her desires, particularly as it was accompanied by a snug little income of two hundred dollars a year, a meagre sum that seemed to open up mysterious avenues of joy to her starved, impatient heart.

When she was a mere infant, her brother was holding her on his knee before the great old-fashioned fireplace heaped with burning logs. A sudden noise startled him, and the crowing, restless baby gave an unexpected lurch, and slipped, face downward, into the glowing embers. It was a full minute before the horror-stricken boy could extricate the little creature from the cruel flame that had already done its fatal work. The baby escaped with her life, but was disfigured for ever. As she grew older, the gentle hand of time could not entirely efface the terrible scars. One cheek was wrinkled and crimson, while one eye and the mouth were drawn down pathetically. The accident might have changed the disposition of any child, but Lyddy chanced to be a sensitive, introspective bit of feminine humanity, in whose memory the burning flame was never quenched. Her mother, partly to conceal her own wounded vanity, and partly to shield the timid, morbid child, kept her out of sight as much as possible; so that at sixteen, when she was left an orphan, she had lived almost entirely in solitude.

She became, in course of time, a kind of general nursery governess in a large family of motherless children. The father was almost always away from home; his sister kept the house, and Lyddy stayed in the nursery, bathing the babies and putting them to bed, dressing them in the morning, and playing with them in the safe privacy of the garden or the open attic.

They loved her, disfigured as she was—for the child despises mere externals, and explores the heart of things to see whether it be good or evil—but they could never induce her to see strangers, nor to join any gathering of people.

The children were grown and married now, and Lyddy was nearly forty when she came into possession of house and lands and fortune; forty, with twenty years of unexpended feeling pent within her. Forty—that is rather old to be interesting, but age is a relative matter. Haven't you seen girls of four-and-twenty who have nibbled and been nibbled at ever since they were sixteen, but who have neither caught anything nor been caught? They are old, if you like, but Lyddy was forty and still young, with her susceptibilities cherished, not dulled, and with all the "language of passion fresh and rooted as the lovely leafage about a spring."

IV

> "He shall daily joy dispense
> Hid in song's sweet influence."
>
> EMERSON'S *Merlin*.

LYDDY had very few callers during her first month as a property owner in Edgewood. Her appearance would have been against her winning friends easily in any case, even if she had not acquired the habits of a recluse. It took a certain amount of time, too, for the community to get used to the fact that old Mrs. Butterfield was dead, and her niece Lyddy Ann living in the cottage on the river road. There were numbers of people who had not yet heard that old Mrs. Butterfield had bought the house from the Thatcher boys, and that was fifteen years ago; but this was not strange, for, notwithstanding Aunt Hitty's valuable services in disseminating general information, there was a man living on the Bonny Eagle road who was surprised to hear that Daniel Webster was dead, and complained that folks were not so long-lived as they used to be.

Aunt Hitty thought Lyddy a Goth and a Vandal because she took down the twenty silver coffin-plates and laid them reverently away. "Mis' Butterfield would turn in her grave," she said, "if she could see her niece. She ain't much of a housekeeper, I guess," she went on, as she cut over Dr. Berry's old trousers into briefer ones for Tommy Berry. "She gives considerable stuff to her hens that she'd a sight better heat over and eat herself, in these hard times, when the missionary societies can't hardly keep the heathen fed and clothed and warmed—no, I don't mean warmed, for most o' the heathens live in hot climates, somehow or 'nother. My back door's jest opposite hers; it's across the river, to be sure, but it's the narrer part, and I can see everything she does as plain as daylight. She washed a Monday, and she ain't taken her clothes in yet, and it's Thursday. She may be bleachin' of 'em out, but it looks slack. I said to Si last night I should stand it till 'bout Friday—seein' 'em lay on the grass there—but if she didn't take 'em in then, I should go over and offer to help her. She has a fire in the settin'-room 'most every night, though we ain't had a frost yet; and as near's I can make out, she's got full red curtains hangin' up to her windows. I ain't sure, for she don't open the blinds in that room till I get away in the morning, and she shuts 'em before I get back at night. Si don't know red from green, so he's useless in such matters. I'm going home late to-night, and walk down on that side o' the river, so 't I can call in after dark and see what makes her house light up as if the sun was settin' inside of it."

As a matter of fact, Lyddy was revelling in house-furnishing of a humble sort. She had a passion for colour. There was a red-and-white straw matting on the sitting-room floor. Reckless in the certain possession of twenty dollars a month, she purchased yards upon yards of turkey red cotton; enough to cover a mattress for the high-backed settle, for long curtains at the windows, and for cushions to the rocking-chairs. She knotted white fringes for the table-covers and curtains, painted the inside of the fireplace red, put some pots of scarlet geraniums on the window-sills, filled a wall-pocket with ferns and tacked it over an ugly spot in the plastering, edged her work-basket with a tufted trimming of scarlet wool, and made an elaborate photograph case of white crash and red cotton that stretched the entire length of the old-fashioned mantelshelf, and held pictures of Mr. Reynolds, Miss Elvira Reynolds, George, Susy, Anna, John, Hazel, Ella, and Rufus Reynolds, her former charges. When all this was done, she lighted a little blaze on the hearth, took the red curtains from their bands, let them fall gracefully to the floor, and sat down in her rocking-chair, reconciled to her existence for absolutely the first time in her forty years.

I hope Mrs. Butterfield was happy enough in Paradise to appreciate and feel Lyddy's joy. I can even believe she was glad to have died, since her dying could bring such content to any wretched living human soul. As Lydia sat in the firelight, the left side of her poor face in shadow, you saw that she was distinctly harmonious. Her figure, clad in a plain black-and-white print dress, was a graceful, womanly one. She had beautifully sloping shoulders and a sweet waist.

Her hair was soft and plentiful, and her hands were fine, strong, and sensitive. This possibility of rare beauty made her scars and burns more pitiful, for if a cheap chromo has a smirch across its face, we think it a matter of no moment, but we deplore the smallest scratch or blur on any work of real art.

Lydia felt a little less bitter and hopeless about life when she sat in front of her own open fire, after her usual twilight walk. It was her habit to wander down the wooded road after her simple five-o'clock supper, gathering ferns or goldenrod or frost flowers for her vases; and one night she heard, above the rippling of the river, the strange, sweet, piercing sound of Anthony Croft's violin.

She drew nearer, and saw a middle-aged man sitting in the kitchen doorway, with a lad of ten or twelve years leaning against his knees. She could tell little of his appearance, save that he had a fine forehead, and hair that waved well back from it in rather an unusual fashion. He was in his shirt-sleeves, but the gingham was scrupulously clean, and he had the uncommon refinement of a collar and necktie. Out of sight herself, Lyddy drew near enough to hear; and this she did every night without recognising that the musician was blind. The music had a curious effect upon her. It was a hitherto unknown influence in her life, and it interpreted her, so to speak, to herself. As she sat on the bed of brown pine needles, under a friendly tree, her head resting against its trunk, her eyes half closed, the tone of Anthony's violin came like a heavenly message to a tired, despairing soul. Remember that in her secluded existence she had heard only such harmony as Elvira Reynolds evoked from her piano or George Reynolds from his flute, and the Reynolds temperament was distinctly inartistic.

Lyddy lived through a lifetime of emotion in these twilight concerts. Sometimes she was filled with an exquisite melancholy from which there was no escape; at others, the ethereal purity of the strain stirred her heart with a strange, sweet vision of mysterious joy; joy that she had never possessed, would never possess; joy whose bare existence she never before realised. When the low notes sank lower and lower with their soft wail of delicious woe, she bent forward into the dark, dreading that something would be lost in the very struggle of listening; then, after a pause, a pure human tone would break the stillness, and soaring, birdlike, higher and higher, seem to mount to heaven itself, and, "piercing its starry floors," lift poor scarred Lydia's soul to the very gates of infinite bliss. In the gentle moods that stole upon her in those summer twilights she became a different woman, softer in her prosperity than she had ever been in her adversity; for some plants only blossom in sunshine. What wonder if to her the music and the musician became one? It is sometimes a dangerous thing to fuse the man and his talents in this way; but it did no harm here, for Anthony Croft was his music, and the music was Anthony Croft. When he played on his violin, it was as if the miracle of its fashioning were again enacted; as if the bird on the quivering bough, the mellow sunshine streaming through the lattice of green leaves, the tinkle of the woodland stream, spoke in every tone; and more than this, the hearth-glow in whose light the patient hands had worked, the breath of the soul bending itself in passionate prayer for perfection, these, too, seemed to have wrought their blessed influence on the willing strings until the tone was laden with spiritual harmony. One might indeed have sung of this little red violin—that looked to Lyddy, in the sunset glow, as if it were veneered with rubies—all that Shelley sang of another perfect instrument:

> "The artist who this viol wrought
> To echo all harmonious thought,
> Fell'd a tree, while on the steep
> The woods were in their winter sleep,
> Rock'd in that repose divine
> Of the wind-swept Apennine;
> And dreaming, some of Autumn past,
> And some of Spring approaching fast,
> And some of April buds and showers,

> And some of songs in July bowers,
> And all of love; and so this tree—
> O that such our death may be!—
> Died in sleep, and felt no pain,
> To live in happier form again."

The viol "whispers in enamoured tone":

> "Sweet oracles of woods and dells,
> And summer winds in sylvan cells; . . .
> The clearest echoes of the hills,
> The softest notes of falling rills,
> The melodies of birds and bees,
> The murmuring of summer seas,
> And pattering rain, and breathing dew,
> And airs of evening; all it knew . . .
> —All this it knows, but will not tell
> To those who cannot question well
> The spirit that inhabits it; . . .
> But, sweetly as its answers will
> Flatter hands of perfect skill,
> It keeps its highest, holiest tone
> For one beloved Friend alone."

Lyddy heard the violin and the man's voice as he talked to the child—heard them night after night; and when she went home to the little brown house to light the fire on the hearth and let down the warm red curtains, she fell into sweet, sad reveries; and when she blew out her candle for the night, she fell asleep and dreamed new dreams, and her heart was stirred with the rustling of new-born hopes that rose and took wing like birds startled from their nests.

V

> "Nor scour the seas, nor sift mankind,
> A poet or a friend to find:
> Behold, he watches at the door!
> Behold his shadow on the floor!"
>
> EMERSON'S *Saadi*.

LYDDY BUTTERFIELD'S hen turkey was of a roving disposition. She had never appreciated her luxurious country quarters in Edgewood, and was seemingly anxious to return to the modest back yard in her native city. At any rate, she was in the habit of straying far from home, and the habit was growing upon her to such an extent that she would even lead her docile little gobblers down to visit Anthony Croft's hens and share their corn.

Lyddy had caught her at it once, and was now pursuing her to that end for the second time. She paused in front of the house, but there were no turkeys to be seen. Could they have wandered up the hill road—the discontented, "traipsing," exasperating things? She started in that direction, when she heard a crash in the Croft kitchen, and then the sound of a boy's voice coming from an inner room—a weak and querulous voice, as if the child were ill.

She drew nearer, in spite of her dread of meeting people, or above all of intruding, and saw Anthony Croft standing over the stove, with an expression of utter helplessness on his usually placid face. She had never really seen him before in the daylight, and there was something about his appearance that startled her. The teakettle was on the floor, and a sea of water was flooding the man's feet, yet he seemed to be gazing into vacancy. Presently he stooped, and fumbled gropingly for the kettle. It was too hot to be touched with impunity, and he finally left it in a despairing sort of way, and walked in the direction of a shelf, from under which a row of coats was hanging. The boy called again in a louder and more insistent tone, ending in a whimper of restless pain. This seemed to make the man more nervous than ever. His hands went patiently over and over the shelf, then paused at each separate nail.

"Bless the poor dear!" thought Lyddy. "Is he trying to find his hat, or what is he trying to do? I wonder if he is music mad?" and she drew still nearer the steps.

At this moment he turned and came rapidly toward the door. She looked straight in his face. There was no mistaking it: he was blind. The magician who had told her, through his violin, secrets that she had scarcely dreamed of, the wizard who had set her heart to throbbing and aching and longing as it had never throbbed and ached and longed before, the being who had worn a halo of romance and genius to her simple mind, was stone blind! A wave of impetuous anguish, as sharp and passionate as any she had ever felt for her own misfortunes, swept over her soul at the spectacle of the man's helplessness. His sightless eyes struck her like a blow. But there was no time to lose. She was directly in his path: if she stood still he would certainly walk over her, and if she moved he would hear her, so, on the spur of the moment, she gave a nervous cough and said, "Good-morning, Mr. Croft."

He stopped short. "Who is it?" he asked.

"I am—it is—I am—your new neighbour," said Lyddy, with a trembling attempt at cheerfulness.

"Oh, Miss Butterfield! I should have called up to see you before this if it hadn't been for the boy's sickness. But I am a good-for-nothing neighbour, as you have doubtless heard. Nobody expects anything of me."

("Nobody expects anything of me." Her own plaint, uttered in her own tone!)

"I don't know about that," she answered swiftly. "You've given me, for one, a great deal of pleasure with your wonderful music. I often hear you as you play after supper, and it has kept me from being lonesome. That isn't very much, to be sure."

"You are fond of music, then?"

"I didn't know I was; I never heard any before," said Lyddy simply; "but it seems to help people to say things they couldn't say for themselves, don't you think so? It comforts me even to hear it, and I think it must be still more beautiful to make it."

Now, Lyddy Ann Butterfield had no sooner uttered this commonplace speech than the reflection darted through her mind like a lightning flash that she had never spoken a bit of her heart out like this in all her life before. The reason came to her in the same flash: she was not being looked at; her disfigured face was hidden. This man, at least, could not shrink, turn away, shiver, affect indifference, fix his eyes on hers with a fascinated horror, as others had done. Her heart was divided between a great throb of pity and sympathy for him and an irresistible sense of gratitude for herself. Sure of protection and comprehension, her lovely soul came out of her poor eyes and sat in the sunshine. She spoke her mind at ease, as we utter sacred things sometimes under cover of darkness.

"You seem to have had an accident; what can I do to help you?" she asked.

"Nothing, thank you. The boy has been sick for some days, but he seems worse since last night. Nothing is in its right place in the house, so I have given up trying to find anything, and am just going to Edgewood to see if somebody will help me for a few days."

"Uncle Tony! Uncle To-ny! where are you? Do give me another drink, I'm so hot!" came the boy's voice from within.

"Coming, laddie! I don't believe he ought to drink so much water, but what can I do? He is burning up with fever."

"Now look here, Mr. Croft," and Lydia's tone was cheerfully decisive. "You sit down in that rocker, please, and let me command the ship for a while. This is one of the cases where a woman is necessary. First and foremost, what were you hunting for?"

"My hat and the butter," said Anthony meekly, and at this unique combination they both laughed. Lyddy's laugh was particularly fresh, childlike, and pleased; one that would have astonished the Reynolds children. She had seldom laughed heartily since little Rufus had cried and told her she frightened him when she twisted her face so.

"Your hat is in the wood-box, and I'll find the butter in the twinkling of an eye, though why you want it now is more than—My patience, Mr. Croft, your hand is burned to a blister!"

"Don't mind me. Be good enough to look at the boy and tell me what ails him; nothing else matters much."

"I will with pleasure, but let me ease you a little first. Here's a rag that will be just the thing," and Lyddy, suiting the pretty action to the mendacious word, took a good handkerchief from her pocket and tore it in three strips, after spreading it with tallow from a candle heated over the stove. This done, she bound up the burned hand skilfully, and, crossing the dining-room, disappeared within the little chamber door beyond. She came out presently, and said half hesitatingly, "Would you—mind—going out in the orchard for an hour or so? You seem to be rather in the way here, and I should like the place to myself, if you'll excuse me for saying so. I'm ever so much more capable than Mrs. Buck; won't you give me a trial, sir? Here's your violin and your hat. I'll call you if you can help or advise me."

"But I can't let a stranger come in and do my housework," he objected. "I can't, you know, though I appreciate your kindness all the same."

"I am your nearest neighbour, and your only one, for that matter," said Lyddy firmly; "it's nothing more than right that I should look after that sick child, and I must do it. I haven't got a thing to do in my own house. I am nothing but a poor lonely old maid, who's been used to children all her life, and likes nothing better than to work over them."

A calm settled upon Anthony's perturbed spirit, as he sat under the apple-trees and heard Lyddy going to and fro in the cottage. "She isn't any old maid," he thought; "she doesn't step like one; she has soft shoes and a springy walk. She must be a very handsome woman, with a hand like that; and such a voice!—I knew the moment she spoke that she didn't belong in this village."

As a matter of fact, his keen ear had caught the melody in Lyddy's voice, a voice full of dignity, sweetness, and reserve power. His sense of touch, too, had captured the beauty of her hand, and held it in remembrance—the soft palm, the fine skin, supple fingers, smooth nails, and firm round wrist. These charms would never have been noted by any seeing man in Edgewood, but they were revealed to Anthony Croft while Lyddy, like the good Samaritan, bound up his wounds. It is these saving stars that light the eternal darkness of the blind.

Lyddy thought she had met her Waterloo when, with arms akimbo, she gazed about the Croft establishment, which was a scene of desolation for the moment. Anthony's cousin from Bridgton was in the habit of visiting him every two months for a solemn house-cleaning, and Mrs. Buck from Pleasant River came every Saturday and Monday for baking and washing. Between times Davy and his uncle did the housework together; and although it was respectably done, there was no pink-and-white daintiness about it, you may be sure.

Lyddy came out to the apple-trees in about an hour, laughing nervously as she said, "I'm sorry to have taken a mean advantage of you, Mr. Croft, but I know everything you have in your house, and exactly where it is. I couldn't help it, you see, when I was making things tidy. It would do you good to look at the boy. His room was too light, and the flies were devouring him. I swept him and dusted him, put on clean sheets and pillow-slips, sponged him with bay rum, brushed his hair, drove out the flies, and tacked a green curtain up to the window. Fifteen minutes after he was sleeping like a kitten. He has a sore throat and considerable fever. Could you—can you—at least, will you, go up to my house on an errand?"

"Certainly I can. I know it inside and out as well as my own."

"Very good. On the clock shelf in the sitting-room there is a bottle of sweet spirits of nitre; it's the only bottle there, so you can't make any mistake. It will help until the doctor comes. I wonder you didn't send for him yesterday?"

"Davy wouldn't have him," apologised his uncle.

"*Wouldn't* he?" inquired Lyddy with cheerful scorn. "He has you under pretty good control, hasn't he? But children are unmerciful tyrants."

"Couldn't you coax him into it before you go home?" asked Anthony in a wheedling voice.

"I can try; but it isn't likely I can influence him, if you can't. Still, if we both fail, I really don't see what's to prevent our sending for the doctor in spite of him. He is as weak as a baby, you know, and can't sit up in bed: what could he do? I will risk the consequences, if you will!"

There was a note of such amiable and winning sarcasm in all this, such a cheery, invincible courage, such a friendly neighbourliness and co-operation, above all, such a different tone from any he was accustomed to hear in Edgewood, that Anthony Croft felt warmed through to the core.

As he walked quickly along the road, he conjured up a vision of autumn beauty from the few hints nature gave even to her sightless ones on this glorious morning—the rustle of a few fallen leaves under his feet, the clear wine of the air, the full rush of the swollen river, the whisking of the squirrels in the boughs, the crunch of their teeth on the nuts, the spicy odour of the apples lying under the trees. He missed his mother that morning more than he had missed her for years. How neat she was, how thrifty, how comfortable, and how comforting! His life was so dreary and aimless; and was it the best or the right one for Davy, with his talent and dawning ambition? Would it not be better to have Mrs. Buck live with them altogether, instead of coming twice a week, as heretofore? No; he shrank from that with a hopeless aversion born of Saturday and Monday dinners in her company. He could hear her pour her coffee into the saucer; hear the scraping of the cup on the rim, and know that she was setting it sloppily down on the cloth. He could remember her noisy drinking, the weight of her elbow on the table, the creaking of her dress under the pressure of superabundant flesh. Besides, she had tried to scrub his favourite violin with sapolio. No, anything was better than Mrs. Buck as a constancy.

He took off his hat unconsciously as he entered Lyddy's sitting-room. A gentle breeze blew one of the full red curtains towards him till it fluttered about his shoulders like a frolicsome, teasing hand. There was a sweet pungent odour of pine-boughs, a canary sang in the window, the clock was trimmed with a blackberry vine; he knew the prickles, and they called up to his mind the glowing tints he had loved so well. His sensitive hand, that carried a divining rod in every finger-tip, met a vase on the shelf, and, travelling upward, touched a full branch of alder berries tied about with a ribbon. The ribbon would be red; the woman who arranged this room would make no mistake; for in one morning Anthony Croft had penetrated the secret of Lyddy's true personality, and in a measure had sounded the shallows that led to the depths of her nature.

Lyddy went home at seven o'clock that night rather reluctantly. The doctor had said Mr. Croft could sit up with the boy unless he grew much worse, and there was no propriety in her staying longer unless there was danger.

"You have been very good to me," Anthony said gravely, as he shook her hand at parting—"very good."

They stood together on the doorstep. A distant bell called to evening prayer-meeting; the restless murmur of the river and the whisper of the wind in the pines broke the twilight stillness. The long, quiet day together, part of it spent by the sick child's bedside, had brought the two strangers curiously near to each other.

"The house hasn't seemed so sweet and fresh since my mother died," he went on, as he dropped her hand, "and I haven't had so many flowers and green things in it since I lost my eyesight."

"Was it long ago?"

"Ten years. Is that long?"

"Long to bear a burden."

"I hope you know little of burden-bearing?"

"I know little else."

"I might have guessed it from the alacrity with which you took up Davy's and mine. You must be very happy to have the power to make things straight and sunny and wholesome; to breathe your strength into helplessness such as mine. I thank you, and I envy you. Good-night."

Lyddy turned on her heel without a word; her mind was beyond and above words. The sky seemed to have descended upon, enveloped her, caught her up into its heaven, as she rose into unaccustomed heights of feeling, like Elijah in his chariot of fire. She very happy! She with power—power to make things straight and sunny and wholesome! She able to breathe strength into helplessness, even a consecrated, God-smitten helplessness like his! She not only to be thanked, but envied!

Her house seemed strange to her that night. She went to bed in the dark, dreading even the light of a candle; and before she turned down her counterpane she flung herself on her knees, and poured out her soul in a prayer that had been growing, waiting, and waited for, perhaps, for years:

"O Lord, I thank Thee for health and strength and life. I never could do it before, but I thank Thee to-night for life on any terms. I thank Thee for this home; for the chance of helping another human creature, stricken like myself; for the privilege of ministering to a motherless child. Make me to long only for the beauty of holiness, and to be satisfied if I attain to it. Wash my soul pure and clean, and let that be the only mirror in which I see my face. I have tried to be useful. Forgive me if it always seemed so hard and dreary a life. Forgive me if I am too happy because for one short day I have really helped in a beautiful way, and found a friend who saw, because he was blind, the real *me* underneath; the me that never was burned by the fire; the me that isn't disfigured, unless my wicked discontent has done it; the me that has lived on and on and on, starving to death for the friendship and sympathy and love that come to other women. I have spent my forty years in the wilderness, feeding on wrath and bitterness and tears. Forgive me, Lord, and give me one more vision of the blessed land of Canaan, even if I never dwell there."

VI

> "Nor less the eternal poles
> Of tendency distribute souls.
> There need no vows to bind
> Whom not each other seek, but find."
>
> EMERSON'S Celestial Love.

DAVY'S sickness was a lingering one. Mrs. Buck came for two or three hours a day, but Lyddy was the self-installed angel of the house; and before a week had passed the boy's thin arms were around her neck, his head on her loving shoulder, and his cheek pressed against hers. Anthony could hear them talk, as he sat in the kitchen busy at his work. Musical instruments were still brought him to repair, though less frequently than of yore, and he could still make many parts of violins far better than his seeing competitors. A friend and pupil sat by his side in the winter evenings and supplemented his weakness, helping and learning alternately, while his blind master's skill filled him with wonder and despair. The years of struggle for perfection had not been wasted; and though the eye that once detected the deviation of a hair's breadth could no longer tell the true from the false, yet nature had been busy with her divine work of compensation. The one sense stricken with death, she poured floods of new life and vigour into the others. Touch became something more than the stupid, empty grasp of things we seeing mortals know, and in place of the two eyes he had lost he now had ten in every finger-tip. As for odours, let other folk be proud of smelling musk and lavender, but let him tell you by a quiver of the nostrils the various kinds of so-called scentless flowers, and let him bend his ear and interpret secrets that the universe is ever whispering to us who are pent in partial deafness because, forsooth, we see.

He often paused to hear Lydia's low, soothing tones and the boy's weak treble. Anthony had said to him once, "Miss Butterfield is very beautiful, isn't she, Davy? You haven't painted me a picture of her yet. How does she look?"

Davy was stricken at first with silent embarrassment. He was a truthful child, but in this he could no more have told the whole truth than he could have cut off his hand. He was knit to Lyddy by every tie of gratitude and affection. He would sit for hours with his expectant face pressed against the window-pane, and when he saw her coming down the shady road he was filled with a sense of impending comfort and joy.

"No," he said hesitatingly, "she isn't pretty, nunky, but she's sweet and nice and dear. Everything on her shines, it's so clean; and when she comes through the trees, with her white apron and her purple calico dress, your heart jumps, because you know she's going to make everything pleasant. Her hair has a pretty wave in it, and her hand is soft on your forehead; and it's 'most worth while being sick just to have her in the house."

Meanwhile, so truly is "praise our fructifying sun," Lydia bloomed into a hundred hitherto unsuspected graces of mind and heart and speech. A sly sense of humour woke into life, and a positive talent for conversation, latent hitherto because she had never known any one who cared to drop a plummet into the crystal springs of her consciousness. When the violin was laid away, she would sit in the twilight, by Davy's sofa, his thin hand in hers, and talk with Anthony about books and flowers and music, and about the meaning of life too—its burdens and mistakes, and joys and sorrows; groping with him in the darkness to find a clue to God's purposes.

Davy had long afternoons at Lyddy's house as the autumn grew into winter. He read to her while she sewed rags for a new sitting-room carpet, and they played dominoes and checkers together in the twilight before supper-time—suppers that were a feast to the boy, after Mrs. Buck's cookery. Anthony brought his violin sometimes of an evening, and Almira Berry, the next neighbour on the road to the Mills, would drop in and join the little party. Almira used to sing "Auld Robin Gray," "What Will You Do, Love," and "Robin Adair," to the great enjoyment of everybody; and she persuaded Lyddy to buy the old church melodeon, and learn to sing alto in "Oh, Wert Thou in the Cauld Blast," "Gently, Gently Sighs the Breeze," and "I Know a Bank." Nobody sighed for the gaieties and advantages of a great city when, these concerts being over, Lyddy would pass crisp seedcakes and raspberry shrub, doughnuts and cider, or hot popped corn and molasses candy.

"But there, she can afford to," said Aunt Hitty Tarbox; "she's pretty middlin' wealthy for Edgewood. And it's lucky she is, for she 'bout feeds that boy o' Croft's. No wonder he wants her to fill him up, after six years of the Widder Buck's victuals. Aurelia Buck can take good flour and sugar, sweet butter and fresh eggs, and in ten strokes of her hand she can make 'em into something the very hogs'll turn away from. I declare, it brings the tears to my eyes sometimes when I see her coming out of Croft's Saturday afternoons, and think of the stone crocks full of nasty messes she's left behind her for that innocent man and boy to eat up . . . Anthony goes to see Miss Butterfield consid'able often. Of course it's awstensibly to walk home with Davy, or do an errand or something, but everybody knows better. She went down to Croft's pretty nearly every day when his cousin Maria from Bridgton come to house-clean. Maria suspicioned something, I guess. Anyhow, she asked me if Miss Butterfield's two hundred a year was in gov'ment bonds. Anthony's eyesight ain't good, but I guess he could make out to cut cowpons off . . . It would be strange if them two left-overs should take an' marry each other; though, come to think of it, I don't know's 't would neither. He's blind, to be sure, and can't see her scarred face. It's a pity she ain't deaf, so 't she can't hear his everlastin' fiddle. She's lucky to get any kind of a husband; she's too humbly to choose. I declare, she reminds me of a Jack-o'-lantern, though if you look at the back of her, or see her in meetin' with a thick veil on, she's about the best appearin' woman in Edgewood . . . I never seen anybody stiffen up as Anthony has. He had me make him three white shirts and three gingham ones, with collars and cuffs on all of 'em. It seems as if six shirts at one time must mean something out o' the common!"

Aunt Hitty was right; it did mean something out of the common. It meant the growth of an all-engrossing, grateful, divinely tender passion between two love-starved souls. On the one hand, Lyddy, who though she had scarcely known the meaning of love in all her dreary life, yet was as full to the brim of all sweet, womanly possibilities of loving and giving as any pretty woman; on the other, the blind violin maker, who had never loved any woman but his mother, and who was in the direst need of womanly sympathy and affection.

Anthony Croft, being ministered unto by Lyddy's kind hands, hearing her sweet voice and her soft footstep, saw her as God sees, knowing the best; forgiving the worst, like God, and forgetting it, still more like God, I think.

And Lyddy? There is no pen worthy to write of Lyddy. Her joy lay deep in her heart like a jewel at the bottom of a clear pool; so deep that no ripple or ruffle on the surface could disturb the hidden treasure. If God had smitten these two with one hand, he had held out the other in tender benediction.

There had been a scene of unspeakable solemnity when Anthony first told Lyddy that he loved her, and asked her to be his wife. He had heard all her sad history by this time, though not from her own lips, and his heart went out to her all the more for the heavy cross that had been laid upon her. He had the wit and wisdom to put her affliction quite out of the question, and allude only to her sacrifice in marrying a blind man, hopelessly and helplessly dependent on her sweet offices for the rest of his life, if she, in her womanly mercy, would love him and help him bear his burdens.

When his tender words fell upon Lyddy's dazed brain she sank beside his chair, and, clasping his knees, sobbed: "I love you, I cannot help loving you, I cannot help telling you I love you! But you must hear the truth, you have heard it from others, but perhaps they softened it. If I marry you, people will always blame me and pity you. You would never ask me to be your wife if you could see my face; you could not love me an instant if you were not blind."

"Then I thank God unceasingly for my infirmity," said Anthony Croft, as he raised her to her feet.

* * * * *

Anthony and Lyddy Croft sat in the apple orchard, one warm day in late spring.

Anthony's work would have puzzled a casual on-looker. Ten stout wires were stretched between two trees, fifteen or twenty feet apart, and each group of five represented the lines of the musical staff. Wooden bars crossed the wires at regular intervals, dividing the staff into measures. A box with many compartments sat on a stool beside him, and this held bits of wood that looked like pegs, but were in reality whole, half, quarter, and eighth notes, rests, flats, sharps, and the like. These were cleft in such a way that he could fit them on the wires almost as rapidly as his musical theme came to him, and Lyddy had learned to transcribe with pen and ink the music she found in wood and wire. He could write only simple airs in this way, but when he played them on the violin they were transported into a loftier region, such genius lay in the harmony, the arabesque, the delicate lacework of embroidery with which the tune was inwrought; now high, now low, now major, now minor, now sad, now gay, with one thrilling, haunting cadence recurring again and again, to be watched for, longed for, and greeted with a throb of delight.

Davy was reading at the window, his curly head buried in a well-worn Shakespeare opened at "Midsummer Night's Dream." Lyddy was sitting under her favourite pink apple-tree, a mass of fragrant bloom, more beautiful than Aurora's morning gown. She was sewing; lining with snowy lawn innumerable pockets in a square basket that she held in her lap. The pockets were small, the needles were fine, the thread was a length of cobweb. Everything about the basket was small except the hopes that she was stitching into it; they were so great that her heart could scarcely hold them. Nature was stirring everywhere. The seeds were springing in the warm earth. The hens were clucking to their downy chicks just out of the egg. The birds were flying hither and thither in the apple-boughs, and there was one little home of straw so hung that Lyddy could look into it and see the patient mother brooding her nestlings. The sight of her bright eyes, alert for every sign of danger, sent a rush of feeling through Lyddy's veins that made her long to clasp the tiny feathered mother to her own breast.

A sweet gravity and consecration of thought possessed her, and the pink blossoms falling into her basket were not more delicate than the rose-coloured dreams that flushed her soul.

Anthony put in the last wooden peg, and taking up his violin called, "Davy, boy, come out and tell me what this means!"

Davy was used to this; from a wee boy he had been asked to paint the changing landscape of each day, and to put into words his uncle's music.

Lyddy dropped her needle; the birds stopped to listen, and Anthony played.

"It is this apple-orchard in May-time," said Davy; "it is the song of the green things growing, isn't it?"

"What do say, dear?" asked Anthony, turning to his wife.

Love and content had made a poet of Lyddy. "I think Davy is right," she said. "It is a dream of the future, the story of all new and beautiful things growing out of the old. It is full of the sweetness of present joy, but there is promise and hope in it besides. It is as if the Spring was singing softly to herself because she held the baby Summer in her arms."

Davy did not quite understand this, though he thought it pretty; but Lyddy's husband did, and when the boy went back to his books, he took his wife in his arms and kissed her twice—once for herself, and then once again.

Milton Keynes UK
Ingram Content Group UK Ltd.
UKHW041821151124
451262UK00005B/724